The Trou
with D

STRICTLY
NO
ENTRY

EGMONT

For Joanna, Caroline and Rosie –
whose Dad also invents funny things!

The Trouble with DAD

Babette Cole

The trouble with Dad . . .

is his boring job.

If he didn't have such a boring job,

he wouldn't spend all his spare time in
the shed making robots.

Mum nagged
Dad about
the robots.

They all went wrong . . . but that didn't stop him.

He made a robotic grass cutter.

He even made some robots to help in the house.

Mum went mad!

He made a robotic hush-a-bye baby improver

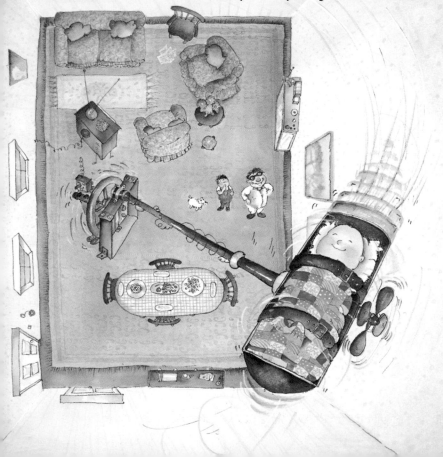

and a robot for seeing old ladies across the road.

Then there was the slimming robot

and the one for catching jewel thieves.

He made a whole football team of robots.
My friend and I challenged them to a match.

They were unbeatable.
They reached the first division!

Dad's robots became famous.

B.B.C.T.V.

They wanted to make a T.V. programme about them.

But before the camera crew could start, my baby brother found . . .

the multi-laser-twister-operator.

When he started it up,
the robots went crazy all over town.

Luckily the little horror dropped it.

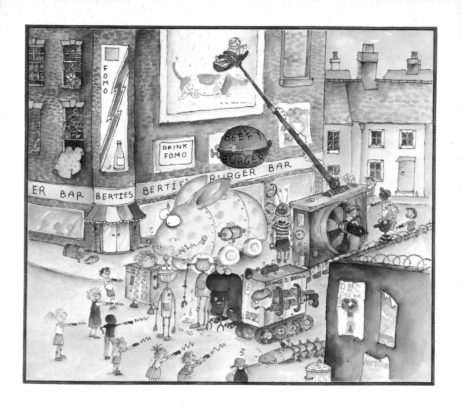

Then my friends and I rounded up
the robots for the programme.

Dad had to pay
for all the damage.

A very rich man saw Dad's robots on the telly.

He bought every single one of them.

Mum was delighted.

He put them in the desert in Arizona.

He called them works of art!

We got rich. Dad didn't have to do his boring
job any more.

Now we both make robots.

First published in Great Britain in 1985
This edition published in 2004
by Egmont Books Limited,
239 Kensington High Street,
London W8 6SA

Text and illustrations copyright © Babette Cole 1985
Babette Cole has asserted her moral rights.
1 3 5 7 9 10 8 6 4 2
1 4052 1122 9
Printed and Bound in Italy

A CIP catalogue record for this title
is available from the British Library